Spell with Zip

 A a

 B b

 C c

 D d

 E e

 F f

 G g

 H h

 I i

 J j

 K k

 L l

 M m

 N n

 O o

 P p

 Q q

 R r

 S s

 T t

 U u

 V v

 W w

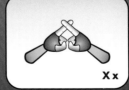 X x

 Y y

 Z z

Zip	Pella	Statz	Goober

Zip is a friendly space alien from planet Zee. He loves to learn. Zip uses his hands to speak to his friends. He can't wait to teach the people of planet Earth all about sign language. Zip is the captain of his spaceship.	Pella is Zip's best friend. She also comes from planet Zee. Pella is very brave. Although she is a little younger than Zip and Statz, she isn't afraid of anything and is always the first of the three friends to try new things.	Statz is in charge of computers on the spaceship. He loves gadgets. Statz uses his Zablet to help him and his friends out of sticky situations. He is excited to learn about planet Earth and all the people who live here.	Goober is an unexpected guest on the friends' adventures. A greedy and naughty space stowaway, Goober has the ability to change his colour and shape so is always jumping out and surprising Zip, Pella and Statz.

Zip's top tips

Zip and friends are here to help you talk in a fun new way - spell with your fingers and talk with your hands. Follow these top tips to get the most from their adventures:

- **Share the book together and enjoy the story**
- **Play with the signs**
- **Use Zip's alphabet to make your own words**
- **Visit Space School, enjoy the activities and have fun**
- **Watch out for Goober...**

Clouds

The spaceship has landed with a splash.

Zip, Pella and Statz look out the window. It is very dull outside, because there are big grey clouds filling the sky. Water is falling from them in droplets and bouncing off the spaceship.

"I've never seen weather like this," says Zip.

Sun

Snow

Wind

Rain

Lightning

Cloudy

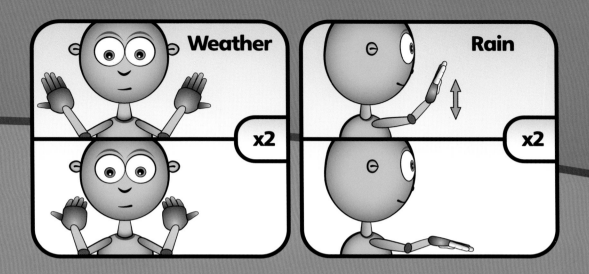

Statz uses his Zablet to look up weather on planet Earth.
There are pages and pages of search results.

"Wow," he says, "there are lots and lots of different types of weather here.
This is rain. It makes everything wet and the ground very muddy."

On planet Zee there is no rain. Sometimes it snows, but the snow is bright green and quite warm, not like the ice cold snow on planet Earth.

Zip, Statz and Pella love to play in the snow. They throw snowballs and build snow-aliens.

Cold

Snow

9

Wind

The three friends don't know what to do with themselves on a rainy day. They can see leaves swirling round in the wind and rain. Zip doesn't want to go outside.

Statz looks up indoor games on his Zablet.
"It says here that Hide and Seek is a good game
to play indoors on a rainy day," he says.

"One player finds a good place to hide. The other
counts to ten and then starts looking," Statz explains.

"I'll hide first," says Zip running off.
"You'll never find me."

Pella and Statz count very slowly.
"We're coming to find you Zip, ready or not!"

They run into the kitchen. "It doesn't look like Zip is here," says Statz. "Where to next?"

Pella and Statz look all over the spaceship for Zip. The sleeping pod, the shower room, the store room, the games room and the control room. They can't find him anywhere.

Zip is very good at hiding. They start going back to rooms they have already tried.

Space School

Take a look at the different types of weather below; you may have seen them in the story. See if you can spell each one using Zip's alphabet.

Back in the kitchen there is a sudden bright flash that lights up the room. Then the friends feel the spaceship shudder.

Zip jumps out of a cupboard. "What was that? Are we under attack?"

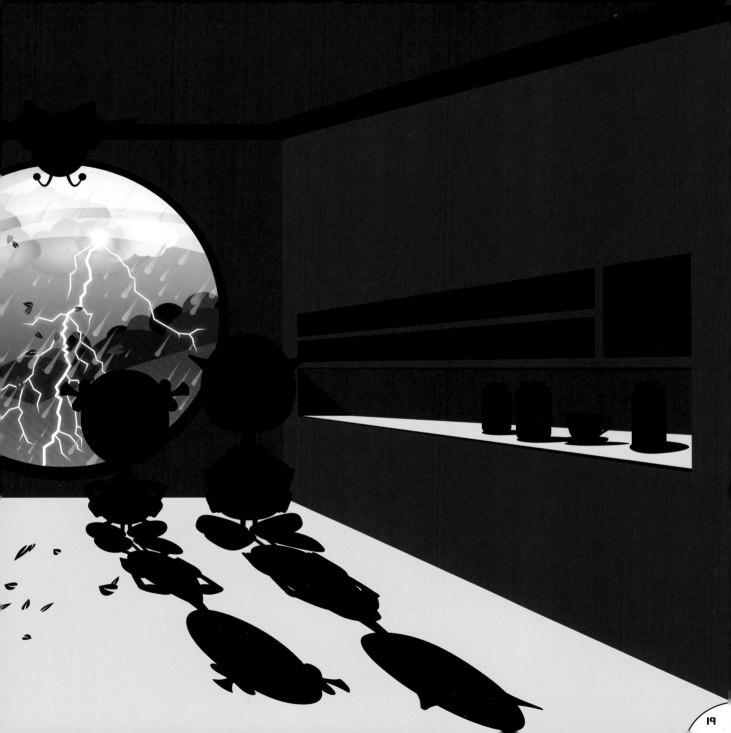

Another flash lights up the sky and the friends run over to the window to take a look.

Zip and Pella are scared. "It's okay," says Statz, "the bright flash was lightning. We're in the middle of a thunderstorm. We are safe in here, there's nothing to worry about."
The friends stand at the window to watch.

"Wow!" says Pella. "Lightning is really exciting."

The spaceship shudders again.
"I don't like thunderstorms," says Zip.

Lightning

Soon the thunderstorm is over and the sun comes out from behind the clouds.

"Hooray! The sun is out," says Pella.

The friends all put on their astro-wellies and run outside.

Pella points up at the sky. "Wow," she says. "That's pretty. What is it?"

"It's a rainbow," says Statz. "They sometimes appear when the sun shines after it has been raining."

The three friends have fun jumping in the puddles.

Rainbow

"I like the weather on planet Earth, it's fun," says Pella.

Zip and Statz both agree as they splash about in the water.

Space School

Take a look at the weather map.
See if you can remember how to sign each of the different types of weather.

The grass dries out quickly in the hot sunshine and the puddles start to disappear one by one until there's only one left. Zip looks at the puddle in amazement. It is big and muddy. It will be great fun to splash around in.

The friends take a long run up and jump high in the air.

They get ready to splash in the water, but land with a bump on the grass.

"Ouch," says Statz. "Where did the puddle go?"

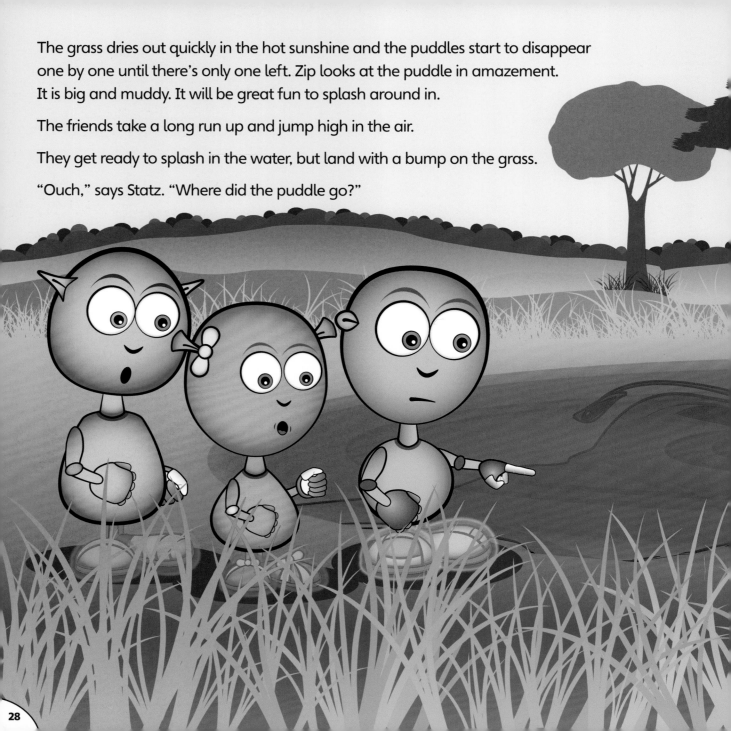

Hot

Zip's Signs

Fun things to do

Now that you have read all about Zip and the Rainy Day,
here are some fun things for you to do:

- Create a game for you and your friends to play
  on a rainy day - draw, describe or make

- Draw your own snow-alien

- How would you feel if you were in the middle
  of a thunderstorm?

- What is your favourite type of weather?

- In a game of hide and seek, where would you hide?

- Teach a friend the sign for today's weather

First published 2013 by Signature

SignSpell® stories created by Signature
Designed and illustrated by Igloo Imaging Ltd.